Dog Farts

Pooter's Revenge

J.B. O'Neil

Published by J.J Fast Publishing, LLC

Dog Farts

Pooter's Revenge

Table of Contents

For my son Joe, who loves to laugh about completely disgusting stuff like boogers, farts, Dutch ovens, wet willies, skid marks, ETC...Enjoy!

FREE BONUS – Dog Farts Audiobook

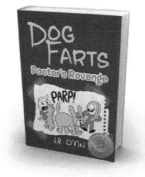

Hey gang...If you'd like to listen to an audiobook version of Dog Farts while you follow along with this book, you can download it for free for a limited time by going online and copying this link: http://funnyfarts.net/dog-farts/

Enjoy!

My Dog Pooter

Nobody makes stinkier, louder, more awesome farts than me. But I must say, my best friend gets pretty close though. He's always ready to rip a juicy butt blaster, and he never gets embarrassed when he makes everybody want to run screaming out of the room. He also loves to sniff people's butts.

OK, I'm talking about my dog, Pooter. I got him when I was just 3 years old and he was a little puppy. All the other puppies at the pound were running, jumping, barking, and playing, but I knew me and Pooter would be best friends because the first thing he did when I saw him was pee on my dad's shoes when he wasn't looking.

Ever since the stone age people and dogs have been together for two reasons: so that dogs could eat, and so that people could blame their farts on somebody else. Pooter knows that's how it goes, so he never gets mad when I pass gas and pass the blame over to him. He's the best dog a boy could ever ask for.

One day though, Pooter got into a lot of trouble and had to get bailed out. It was the least I could do for my best friend, and I'd do it again right now. Not just because I love Pooter, but because it was the funniest day I had since I turned my underwear into a hot-air balloon and floated through the hallways at my school without my pants on.

But that's a story I'll have to tell you about later. Here's what happened on one of the craziest days me and Pooter ever spent together.

Captain Super-Hero Man!

As soon as I woke up on that awesome Saturday morning I ran down stairs and turned on the TV to watch Captain Super-Hero Man. My favorite super-hero was caught in the clutches of The Man With the Spooky Laugh, and I had to know how it ended. Of course, as soon as I turned on the TV Pooter came slouching into the room and fell over on his side next to me on the floor. Pooter isn't a morning dog.

Captain Super-Hero Man was just about to pull something out of his amazing utility belt when my little sister Brittney walked in. She still acts like a baby and cries about a lot of things that really aren't a big deal, like eating vegetables, going to school on the bus, and almost getting flushed down the toilet. (but that's another story for another day).

Anyway, Brittney came into the room and I knew right away that she was going to be an annoying little sister. "I wanna watch TV!" she whined.

"You are watching TV," I said. I mean, she was: she was standing right there, watching the TV!

"I wanna watch something ELSE! You ALWAYS get to watch whatever you want Milo!"

"I'm not changing the channel Brittney," I said, turning my head to ignore her. That's the best thing you can do about little sisters: ignore them until they shut up, or tell on you.

"Why NOT!?" Brittney screamed, but she screamed so loud, she farted.

"That's why! You're such a baby you pooped your pants!" I said.

Pooter's Revenge

"I did not! I'm not a baby!" Brittney said, and she started to cry (just like she always does).

"You are too, farty-baby!" I teased.

"I didn't fart! Pooter did!" Brittney said, stomping her feet and pointing at Pooter.

Pooter just yawned. Then he got up and stretched.

"Farty-baby, farty-baby, farty-poopy-butt-baby!" I sang, and of course that just made Brittney madder. I think she was about ready to go tattle, but then...

Pooter lifted up his tail, put his butt right next to my face, and launched a fart so hot and stinky it squeezed about a gallon of tears out of my eyes. They splashed onto my pants, and you know what that looks like...

"Haha, Milo, you look like you peed in your pants!" Brittney said, giggling. Of course, she wasn't crying at all anymore, the little faker. But I couldn't even say anything, the fart had been so bad I couldn't breathe.

"Milo's a baby, Milo's a baby!" Brittney sang, but then Pooter started wagging his tail. Brittney was about to start doing her "I'm better than my stupid big brother dance" when the fart made it's way over to her. She squealed and clapped her hands over her nose. "AGGH! It burns!" she screamed.

Nothing Like Your Own Brand

I was just ready to turn the tables on Brittney and hopefully finish watching Captain Super-Hero Man when Pooter lifted his tail up again and let out a giant bottom burp that was even worse than the first one. This one was so bad I was glad I hadn't eaten breakfast yet. And the third dog fart was so bad it made Brittney regret that she HAD eaten breakfast!

Farts are great, but farts this bad couldn't be normal. It smelled like rotten fish that an elephant pooped out into a rotten diaper. The room was starting to get wavy and a little green. I couldn't see the TV clearly anymore. I was going to miss Captain Super-Hero Man!

I thought about what a super hero would do, and realized that in this situation, they'd fight fire with fire. Even the worst fart isn't so bad when it's your own brand!

I clenched my butt cheeks and pushed out the biggest, gassiest, most space-taking fart I could. It whistled and hissed as it came out, like I was filling a balloon. The fart expanded and expanded, and I when I looked behind me I could almost see the outline of it, like a wavy gassy bag.

Then it popped, with a huge sound like someone sneezing into a tuba. Suddenly the room smelled exactly the way it should: like Milo Snotrocket's farts.

It's the sweetest air freshener in the world.

Is Pooter OK?

Brittney has been smelling my farts forever, so she was really used to them and didn't mind the new smell as much. But we were still very concerned about the horrible face-melting fart that Pooter had just fired out of his body from under his tail.

"Pooter, are you ok?" She asked, petting Pooter. Pooter sure looked ok. He was wagging his tail and panting, his eyes open as wide as they ever got: sorta half-open and squinty.

"He looks fine to me," I said, shrugging my shoulders. "Pooter farts all the time."

"But he never farts THAT bad," Brittney said, frowning. She actually looked pretty worried. "Maybe he has to go to the vet."

"No way Brittney, he's fine!" I said, but I kind of, sort of, maybe said that to make myself feel better too. The farts WERE bad. In fact they were completely awful! "Everyone gets some toxic gas toots sometimes. Nothing to worry about!"

I turned around so I could keep watching Captain Super-Hero Man on TV. He was about to beat The Man With the Spooky Laugh once and for all! I leaned in close, so excited I was about to pee in my pants for real, and then the television exploded.

I'm not kidding! I heard a loud "BRAPP!" noise, and then the television just blew up. Brittney and I frog-jumped three feet away!

Pooter just looked at us, wagging his tail like nothing had happened. He had just farted so hard he blew up the television. And that's when we knew something was definitely wrong with our dog.

"Um, I think we need to take Pooter to the vet."

Mom, Seriously!

"Mom, Mom!" Me and Brittney started shouting, hurrying to the kitchen. Pooter followed us, his collar jingling like absolutely nothing was weird.

Mom was sitting at the kitchen table, talking to one of her friends from college on the phone.

"Mom!" I screamed.

She ignored us.

"Mom!" Brittney yelled.

She ignored us.

"MOM!" we both hollered.

"Hold on Sheryl," she said, and she gave us the Angry Mom Look. You know the one I'm talking about. It just makes you want to go sit on your bed quietly and hope she never finds you again. Brittney and I were helpless.

"Kids, please! I'm on...the...phone." She stared at us for like 8 seconds with her eyes bugging out of her head. It was completely quiet in the kitchen, and then she started talking on the phone again like nothing had happened.

I looked at Brittney. "You tell her," I whispered.

"Why me, you tell her!" Brittney whispered back.

"Rock paper scissors," I said. I lost.

"Mom, mom!" I said, tugging on her shirt.

"Hang on Sheryl, the kids are acting out a little today," she glared at me. "What is it!?" she snapped.

"Mom, Pooter has to go to the vet! He's farting really, really bad."

"Don't be silly Milo, Pooter is a dog. Dog's fart all the time."

"But Mom, this is different! He blew up the TV with his butt!"

"Don't lie to me Milo," Mom said, "Pooter doesn't need to go to the vet for his farts!"

And right at that moment Pooter let out a deafening butt-trumpet right there in front of my Mom's face. It was so loud the dishes jumped out of the cupboards and smashed onto the kitchen floor. "Oh, o...ewwww!" Mom screamed, holding her nose. On the phone, I could clearly hear Sheryl screaming "What was that!? Why does the phone smell so bad!? What happened!?"

The Dreadful Drive

Mom told Sheryl she'd have to call her back and told us to get our shoes on. We were going to the vet right away because she said this was a medical emergency.

So the four of us jumped into the minivan and started driving. Within five seconds in the car we had to roll all the windows down and stick our heads out the window to breathe. Pooter was totally fine with that: normally he never got to put his head the window when we drove anywhere.

We get on the highway and sped to downtown to get to the vet. I looked behind us and saw that some of the cars were swerving a little. Then suddenly they started crashing!

Within seconds, the highway was backed up with a fifty-car pileup so bad the news crews started flying helicopters overhead to cover it. One of the helicopters started following us! "Mom, turn on the radio!" I said.

"I'm here live via helicopter at the scene of the worst traffic accident in the city's history, and it's only getting worse!" the news reporter said over the radio. "It appears that a single car is causing this incredible devastation, a car belonging to a Mrs. Snotrocket of 123 Fake Street right, here in Poopertown! Mrs. Snotrocket's car smells so bad it's causing people to crash their cars!"

Mom didn't say anything, but she was gripping the steering wheel so hard that it looked like he fingernails were stuck in it.

Cut the Cheese, Cut the Line

When we got to the vet's office, it was completely jam-packed with pets and owners. "Oh, this is just great!" Mom snapped. "It's going to take hours to get see the vet!"

We couldn't even sit down, so we just stood waiting in line behind about ten other people. Pooter seemed to be having a good time though: all the other dogs were sniffing his butt and wagging their tails. It almost seemed like they were really impressed at what was shoot out of his dog-butt.

One little fuzzy dog was just getting a really good whiff of Pooter's poo-hole when he fired a butt-pedo that knocked the little dog over. Suddenly all the people in the room were gagging and coughing.

"Ah! We're under attack! Run!" they screamed, some of them barely managing to cover their mouths so they didn't barf on the floor. They ran away, were probably going to see a people-doctor instead of the animal-doctor now.

In just a few seconds, the office was empty except for my family and the receptionist. She didn't seem to know what to say.

"Um, next patient?"

Veterinary Analysis

We came into the vet's room. She seemed like a nice fat lady, and she was.

"Hi Pooter! Good boy," she said. "What seems to be the trouble?" she said to us, smiling.

"The dog's farting even worse than my son Milo," Mom said. I took a bow: it's not easy being great. "Isn't there anything you can do?"

"Farts, huh? Well, dogs pass gas fairly frequently," she said, lifting Pooter's tail up to take a closer look at his butt. "It's usually nothing to worry about, even if it is stinkier than..."

Right then Pooter fired a fart into the doctor's face. She slowly turned green, then put Pooter's tail down very, very slowly.

She didn't say anything for a little while.

"This is the worst case I have ever seen," she said. Her voice sounded very flat, like someone talking while they're hypnotized. "There is nothing I can do."

Then she turned around, walked out of the room, closed the door, and never came back.

Nothing to Do But Wait

We left the vet's office, even more worried than before. Pooter didn't seem worried though. If anything, all his farting was making him frisky.

Right when we got to the car a gang of news reporters ambushed us.

"Mrs. Snotrocket, Mrs. Snotrocket!" the news people shouted, shoving their microphones into Mom's face, "do you have any comment on the fatally foul flatulence that came out of your car this morning? Do you plan on causing more terror and destruction on the road today?"

"I have a comment!" I shouted. The news reporters and cameras all bent down toward me.

"Hi Mom!" I said, waving.

"Milo, I'm right here," Mom sighed, shoving past the reporters and getting in the car.

"I know Mom, but when this goes on the news tonight, I want you to see me!" I said. Mom didn't reply. She was so mad that I almost expected laser beams to shoot out of her eyeballs and cut me in half.

We left the news reporters behind, drove back onto the highway, and drove home as fast as we could.

When we got home, Pooter stunk up the house so bad we had to put him outside. It was the best we could do, but the stink didn't go away, even when Dad arrived home from work. It turns out that my Mom had called him and told him that someone was really sick and he needed to come home right away.

Dad's Home

I don't know why, but the one thing Dad hates worst in the world is farting. It doesn't make any sense to me, because I'm the biggest farter in the world and I always figured it was genetic somehow.

Mom promises me that I wasn't adopted, but I don't believe her.

So when Dad walked in the front door, he was in a bad mood. When he opened his mouth to complain about work and got a big gulp of fart-gas instead, he got in an even WORSE mood.

"It smells like someone barfed egg salad onto burnt lasagna in here!" He yelled. "Did someone fart? Milo, if you farted, so help me..."

"It wasn't me Dad!" I said. "It's Pooter! He's been farting so bad we had to take him to the vet!"

"Milo, why are you always blaming the dog?" Dad said. "You need to take some responsibility young man!"

Pooter started scratching at the door to get back in to the house. As Dad walked over to the door, we all pleaded with him "No, don't let him in!"

"Don't tell me what to do. This is my house and I'll do whatever I want!" My dad shouted, and as soon as he let Pooter inside the house, he farted on Dad.

Dad screamed. "These are the worst dog farts I've ever smelled! If you don't stop this dog's farting tonight, I'm going to leave him at a dog farm!!"

Gotta Save Pooter!

"Milo, what're we gonna do? Daddy's gonna take Pooter out to a dog farm! I don't even know what that means, but it doesn't sound good." Brittney said, tearing up. A big wet booger was oozing out of her nose.

"No way Brittney, it'll be OK. Come on, let's find out how to stop dog farts on the internet!" I said. Brittney nodded and smiled, snorting the booger bubble back into her nose.

When we got to the computer I suddenly stopped. "What is it Milo?" Brittney asked.

"I just can't believe I'm looking for a way to STOP farts. This goes against everything I believe in..." I said.

We logged onto the computer and started running searches on Foogle.com. When we searched "Dog Fart Cures," we got over 39 million hits!

"Wow, I guess a lot of people have had this problem," I said, moving my mouse over all the links. I didn't know which one to pick.

"Do that one Milo, the news story," Brittney said. I clicked on it, but it wasn't what we wanted to see:

Dog Farts Wipe Out Entire Town

Lack of proven cure for dog farts causes destruction of small town of 80,000

"There's only one thing we can do," I said seriously. "We gotta try every single one of these dog fart cures until we find the one that works."

"Hooray! This is gonna be fun!" Brittney said.

Dog Farts Cure #1: Clean Start

"What's the first one Milo?" Brittney asked.

"Well it says to feed the dog soapy water," I read. "It's supposed to clean the dog's guts out."

"How much soap do we need?"

I thought about it. "At least three or four bars I bet. We should make Pooter eat some sponges and towels too, so he gets REALLY clean inside."

We went into all the bathrooms and took all the soap, then covered the soap in peanut butter (Pooter's favorite snack) and fed them to Pooter. Then we fed him two sponges, a towel, a dish-scrubber, and a rubber ducky.

The second sponge didn't seem to go down as well as the other stuff, and soon Pooter was looking a little sick.

"Oh man, he's gonna barf!" I said, and right then Pooter hurled up everything in a sticky-brown bubbly mess.

"Ewwww!" Brittney said, "he got it on Mom's favorite rug!"

Just then Pooter lifted up his tail. "Oh man, he's gonna fart!" I said.

Instead of a loud "BRRRAPP!" and a cloud of stink though, Pooter silently shot about a hundred green bubbles out of his butt. Some were big, some were small, and they were floating around the room everywhere.

"Oooh, hey, they're pretty!" Brittney said.

Then they started popping, and every time they popped, they let out a little "PHBT!" and a cloud of stinky fart.

Dog Farts Cure #2:
Plug the Butt

"OK, that didn't go so well," I said. "The next one is easy: it says if we just stop up Pooter's butt hole, then the farts will get stuck inside him until they go away!"

"What can we use to plug Pooter's butt?" Brittney wondered.

I thought about it. "Let's grab that big cork out of that old wine bottle Mom and Dad have in the kitchen!"

"I thought they said they were saving it for their anniversary?" Brittney said.

"Don't be a hole-flapper Brittney," I said. I grabbed the bottle from the kitchen and got the corkscrew. I had to really twist the corkscrew hard, and I had to pull it a lot, but finally I got the cork out with a loud "Pop!"

"Milo, you spilled the wine on the carpet," Brittney whined.

"Mom and Dad care more about Pooter than a dumb carpet. Besides, maybe the wine will help clean up the dog barf," I said. I walked around to Pooter's butt.

"OK boy, I don't think you're gonna like this, but here goes nothing!" I said, and shoved the cork into Pooter's butt.

Pooter yelped and spun around in the air. It scared a little fart scream out of me, but only a little one (I don't get scared easily).

"Ok boy, good dog. I think everything's going to be OK now," I said, patting Pooter on the head.

"Woof!" Pooter barked, and then lifted his tail up. Then the cork suddenly fired out of Pooter's butt like a rocket, and started smashing around the room. It smashed Mom's favorite vase, cracked the glass on dad's old clock, and shattered a bunch of little glass toys Mom calls "heirlooms" (whatever that means).

"OK smart guys, what's next?" Brittney asked.

Dog Farts Cure #3: Catch 'em All!

"Next we're going to neutralize the farts out by capturing them in bottles," I said.

"We only have one bottle," Brittney said, pointing at the wine bottle that was slowly spilling wine into a bigger and bigger puddle on the rug. "We'll need more than that, right?"

"Right. We gotta chug some soda and collect the bottles, Brittney," I said. We went to the fridge in the kitchen and got out twelve plastic bottles of soda.

"You ready little sis? Time to CHUG!" I said.

We chugged six bottles of soda each.

"OK Brittney **BURP** we have to **URP** catch Pooter's **URAAP** farts now," I said, feeling a little gassy.

"Big **BRAAA**ther," Brittney said, "I don't **FEELRP** so good."

"**BRAAP** we have to save Pooter **BUUUR**ittny," I replied, bravely waddling into the living room where Pooter was waiting.

We started collecting Pooter's farts into bottles, but meanwhile, we couldn't stop burping.

Fart, burp, fart, burp, fart fart fart, burp burp burp, fartburp, furp, bart...

We filled all twelve soda bottles and the wine bottle with Pooter's farts, but Pooter still wasn't done farting. We left the fart bottles by the front door to throw out later.

We stopped burping though, which is too bad. As I always say: a fart is just a burp turned upside-down.

"I think we did it Milo! Pooter stopped farting!" Brittney asked.

Of course, as soon as she said this, the dog pushed one of the hugest and stinkiest dog farts

I'd ever experienced at close range...right in my face in fact.

Brittney and I both knew we needed to find something that worked fast, or Dad was going to get rid of Pooter!

Dog Farts Cure #4: Sweet Music

"OK Brittney," I said as I sat down at the computer again. "Here's the next cure: slow, gentle music."

"How about Daddy's opera?" Brittney suggested.

We grabbed some of Dad's CD's and took them into his study with the dog. This was where Dad goes when he's cranky.

"Oh no you don't," he said as we came in. "I've been hearing your awful racket all day, and you're not bringing that dog in here to stink the place up!"

"Don't worry dad," I said as I put a CD in Dad's CD player and pressed the "Play" button. "I think you'll like this next cure."

Soon the boring sounds of opera singers and about a hundred violins filled Dad's study.

"Ahhh..." Dad said, slowly closing his eyes and letting out a big sigh, "Hey, this cure isn't bad. In fact this is the best one yet. And I think it's working!"

Brittney and I winked at each other. This plan was perfect.

And then we heard it..."Fart".

"Uh oh, it's not working," Brittney whispered as she looked down at Pooter, who was wagging his tail and looking back up at us.

"Fart, fart, fart!" Wag, wag, wag.

Dad's eyes snapped open. They were a little bloodshot now. "Get that dog out of my office NOW!" he hollered.

Dad Loses His Marbles

"I can't take it anymore!" Dad screamed, ripping his newspaper into a thousand pieces of confetti and throwing it in the air. "I have to get out of here, these dog farts are driving me crazy!"

He stomped out of his study into the living room, while Brittney, Pooter, and I stayed in the study.

"Has Daddy gone crazy Milo?" Brittney said.

"Not yet Brittney. But soon," I said.

"AGGHH! Who did this!? Who spilled wine all over the rug? Who left all these bathroom tools on the rug!?!??!? It smells like barf!!!"

We came out of the study just in time to see Dad storming to the front door.

"I have to go for a drive, I just can't deal with all of this right now!" Dad said, but not to anyone in the room as far as I could tell. He saw the capped soda bottles next to the door and grabbed one.

"No wait, Dad..." I said, but it was too late. Dad unscrewed the cap and took a big drink of fart.

"UURRGHH!" he groaned, and he dropped the bottle. "Farts...farts, they're everywhere! All the farts, leave me alone farts!" He stumbled and mumbled out the front door. Pooter ran after him, and Brittney and I followed right after them.

"Go for a drive, run from the farts," Dad mumbled and giggled to himself as he got in his car. "No farts here, no farts, no," he started the car...

And just as he did, Pooter farted into Dad's exhaust pipe.

"I HATE FARTS!!" Dad screamed, as the fart caught fire in the hot engine and turned his car into a rocket. Me and Brittney watched his car sail up, up, up into the sky, and out of sight. A few seconds later, we heard a big splash. I think he crashed into the lake on the other side of town.

We both looked at each other, as if to say "What the heck just happened?"

Then we knew there was only one thing left to do. "Back to the computer Britt!" I said, and we marched back inside to solve Pooter's terrible farts.

Dog Farts Cure #5: Fart-o-Copter

"But Milo, it's almost dinner time!" Brittney said after we got back to the computer. "As soon as Dad gets back he's going to take Pooter to the dog farm and we'll never see him again because he won't stop farting!"

"I think dad's got bigger problems right now Brittney," I said, searching for another dog-fart cure that looked like it actually might work. "OK, here's a good one: get the dog to spin around in circles and centrifugal force will push the farts out!"

"What's centrifugal force?" Brittney asked.

"Beats me, you were the one that sounded like a science teacher earlier," I replied.

"No I didn't."

"Never mind...we have to focus Brittney!" I said. I went over to Pooter, and spread some fresh peanut butter on the very end of his long hairy tail.

"Look Pooter, look!" I said, picking up Pooter's tail and wagging it at his face. Pooter got really quiet and followed his tail, moving back and forth, back and forth...

"BARK BARK BARK BARK!" said Pooter, and all of a sudden he started chasing his tail.

Pooter ran faster and faster, and his tail ran away even faster and faster. Soon Pooter was a spinning so fast I couldn't really see him anymore.

Then he let out a fart.

"It's working!" I yelled. Then he let out a bunch more.

"It's really working!" I yelled, jumping up and down with happiness. Then the fart gases started to swirl around Pooter as he kept farting.

"I don't really know what's happening," I said, taking a step back. Pooter began to rise up into the air in a swirling storm of fart.

"It's not working anymore!" I cried. Pooter began to fly through the air, crashing into everything in the house.

"Run for your lives! It's a fart-o-copter!" I screamed.

Dad's Home Again

I was sure that Pooter the fart-o-copter was going to destroy the house and possibly go on an unstoppable tuba-tooting rampage, but right then Dad got home. He slammed the door shut so hard it created a giant gust of wind that blew the farts away. Pooter slowly dropped down to the ground, his eyes rolling around in his head but otherwise OK.

Dad splashed into the living room. He was soaking wet and had a fish in his pants.

"I... have had...a VERY...bad day, Milo," Dad said to me.

"I'll say Dad. You smell like fish," I said, pinching my nose shut.

"I just want three things: quiet, dinner, and no more farts from that dog! No more farting Milo, do you understand me? Are we clear about this Milo? IS IT SO MUCH TO ASK FOR JUST ONE DAY WITHOUT FARTING?"

I knew dad wanted me to agree, and even though I love farts more than anything else, I decided to give him the win just this one time. I nodded slowly and carefully.

He let his shoulders sag down and let out a big sigh. He gently dripped water onto the carpet.

Pooter farted.

Dad screamed.

We were dead meat.

Mystery Solved

OK...Long story short, Brittney and I cleaned up the dog's peanut-butter-barf pile, mopped up the spilled wine, picked up all the broken stuff, threw out the fart bottles, got the fart cloud to rain and let the stinky fart-juice down the bathtub drain, and accepted the fact that we were going to be grounded for the next several hundred years.

That night we all sat at the table together, enjoying a nice family dinner. Dad was still damp and still smelled like fish, and he spent the dinner viciously chopping and stabbing his food instead of eating it. Mom didn't eat anything because she said she had a really bad headache, so she just sat at the table with her head in her hands.

For the first time in my life, I didn't think farts were very funny. My dog's farts had gone too far, and I knew that Dad was getting ready to take Pooter away. I hadn't been able to stop the farts. I picked at my food, but I wasn't very hungry.

Under the table, Pooter farted.

"That does it!" Dad screamed, "There will be no more farts, EVER! That dog is going to the nice farm in the country, FOREVER!" He was so mad that he flipped over the whole table...

And suddenly we could see that Brittney was holding out some green beans to Pooter.

"Brittney, have you been feeding Pooter your green beans this whole time?" Mom asked quietly.

"Uh oh," Brittney said.

All's Well That Ends Well

It really wasn't Brittney's fault. I mean, she was being a big baby about her vegetables as usual, but she's just a kid. She couldn't have known that green beans give dogs incredibly horrible dog farts.

Now that Brittney eats her own vegetables, Pooter has gone back to his old ways, only farting every now and then. Which is great for me, because now I can blame my farts on him again when I can't take credit for them like I want to.

The only problem is, it turns out that Brittney gets some pretty mean green bean farts...in fact, her farts are even worse than Pooter's. In a way, stopping Pooter's farts and getting Brittney to eat her green beans was the worst thing my Dad ever did to himself. I mean, Dad can't take Brittney out to the nice farm in the country-side.

Can he?

MORE FUNNY FARTS...

If you laughed really hard at Dog Farts, I know you'll love these other stinky bestselling books by J.B. O'Neil (for kids of *all* ages!)

http://jjsnip.com/fart-book

And...

http://jjsnip.com/booger-fart-books

Silent but Deadly...As a Ninja Should Be!

http://jjsnip.com/ninja-farts-book

Did you know cavemen farted?

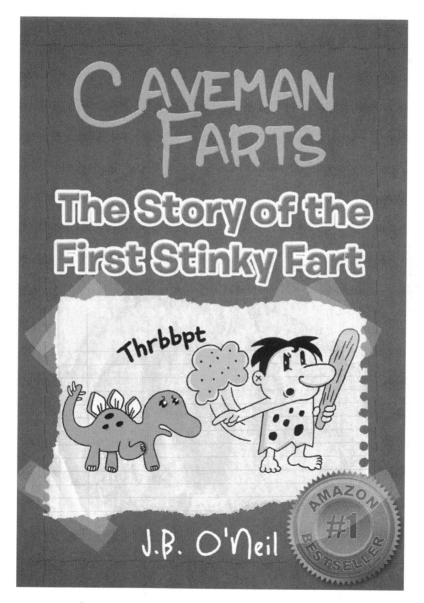

http://jjsnip.com/caveman-farts

A long time ago, in a galaxy fart, fart away...

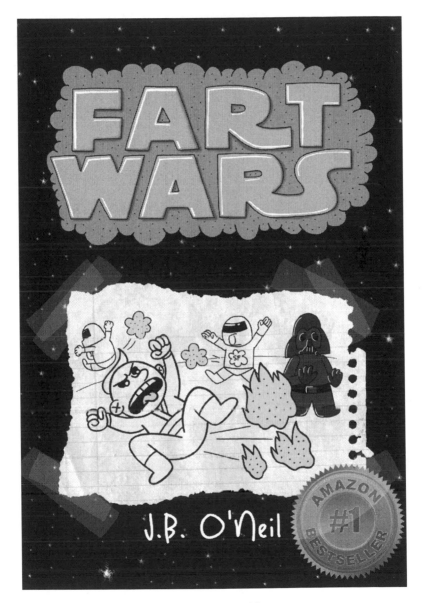

http://jjsnip.com/fart-wars

And check out my new series, the

Family Avengers!

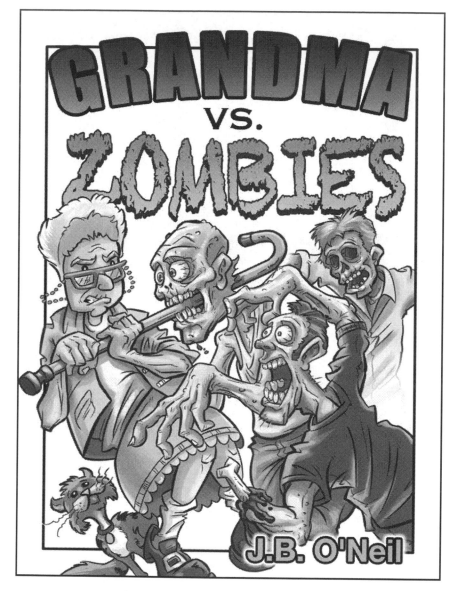

http://jjsnip.com/gvz

Made in the USA
Middletown, DE
02 April 2020